Other books in the
RSPCA ANIMAL TALES series

Ruby's Misadventure

Helen Kelly

RANDOM HOUSE AUSTRALIA

A Random House book
Published by Random House Australia Pty Ltd
Level 3, 100 Pacific Highway, North Sydney NSW 2060
www.randomhouse.com.au

First published by Random House Australia in 2012

Addresses for companies within the Random House Group can be
found at www.randomhouse.com.au/offices

National Library of Australia
Cataloguing-in-Publication Entry

Author:	Kelly, Helen
Title:	Ruby's misadventure / Helen Kelly
ISBN:	978 1 74275 328 7 (pbk)
Series:	Animal tales; 2
Target Audience:	For primary school age
Subjects:	Animals–Juvenile fiction
	Cats–Juvenile fiction
Dewey Number:	A823.4

Cover photograph © Patricia Doyle/Getty Images
Cover and internal design by Ingrid Kwong
Internal illustrations by Charlotte Whitby
Internal photographs: image of cat by iStockphoto; image of horse by
Shutterstock; image of lily by iStockphoto
Typeset by Midland Typesetters, Australia
Printed in Australia by Griffin Press, an accredited ISO AS/NZS
14001:2004 Environmental Management System printer

Random House Australia uses papers that are natural, renewable
and recyclable products and made from wood grown in sustainable
forests. The logging and manufacturing processes are expected to
conform to the environmental regulations of the country of origin.

Chapter One

'Three sleepovers in a row! It's going to be just like we're sisters!' said Sarah.

Sarah was beside herself with excitement and Cassie let her go on without interruption. She was excited too, of course; it was going to be a wonderful few days.

School had finished and the girls were

passing by the park on their way home, just as they did every day. But today was different. Today was the day that they had both been looking forward to for weeks.

Sarah's parents had been married for eleven years and had decided that this year it was time for them to celebrate their wedding anniversary in style. They had booked themselves into a hotel on the beach for three whole days and children were not allowed!

'I still can't believe Mum let me stay here with you, instead of going to Gran's with the boys. It's going to be so quiet without them!' Sarah sighed. 'So, what shall we do first, Cassie? As my older and wiser *sister*, I think you should decide.'

'Mmmm. I am two months older and y'know, that really does make me very, very wise.' Cassie adopted her most thoughtful expression and pondered. 'How about starting with a milkshake?' This was a common suggestion from Cassie. Her mum and dad ran the local deli in Abbotts Hill and made the best milkshakes for miles around.

'Perfect!' agreed Sarah.

'Then we could take Ripper down to the park for a run. You know Mark from school? His family have just adopted a tiny puppy from the RSPCA. He might be there. He's called –'

Cassie came to an abrupt stop. Sarah heard a garbled *aaarghh* and turned around to see her friend flat on the floor with a large black-and-white dog on top of her! Sarah didn't know what to do. But then she realised that Cassie was laughing so hard that she could hardly breathe. Sarah exhaled with relief. Clearly this dog was friend, not foe.

Cassie managed to get herself into a sitting position but was still full of giggles.

'Calm down, Florence! Yes, it's great to see you too. Now sit!'

The dog sat obediently and Cassie managed to get to her feet, straightening her hair, her school-bag and her slobbered-on face all in one smooth movement.

'So this is a friend of yours?' asked Sarah.

'Sarah, meet Florence and –' Cassie glanced back in the direction Florence had come from '– you know Ben Stoppard from school.'

A very embarrassed-looking Ben ran up to them.

'Hi, Ben. Lost something?' asked Cassie.

'No!' He spluttered, staring furtively back the way he'd come. 'No, it's just that Florence got away from me. You know what she's like.'

He was breathless from running across the park. 'She must have seen you. She just took off! Are you okay?' Ben regained his breath and flicked his floppy hair back as he picked up the end of his dog's lead. Florence smiled beautifully at each of them and continued to sit.

'I'm fine!' said Cassie. 'No harm done, though some doggy breath-freshener wouldn't go amiss. Eau de Dog Breath is definitely *not* my favourite fragrance.'

'What are you two up to?' asked Ben as he looked back into the park again.

'We're just heading home for a milkshake,' said Cassie. 'Sarah's staying with me for three days and we have some serious planning to do for tonight!'

'That sounds great!' said Ben. 'What's the flavour of the day?'

Both Cassie and Sarah stopped and stared at him.

'Let me rephrase that for you,' said Cassie. '*Sarah and I* are going home to plan *our super-girly sleepover* over a milkshake. Just so there's no confusion, that is, *a sleepover for girls*, talking about *girl's stuff*. Maybe we'll see you later back here? I promised Mrs Stephens that I'll take Rusty out for a walk.'

Ben was still looking uneasily over his

shoulder and seemed keen to leave the park quickly.

'I'll just join you for the milkshake bit, then. Come on, let's go.'

Ben was behaving very strangely and the girls weren't sure his ears were working properly either. He was definitely up to something.

Cassie and Sarah glanced back into the park to see what he might be avoiding, but could see nothing except a gaggle of small children and lots of dogs.

'Okay,' they agreed. 'But only for the milkshake bit!'

Chapter Two

'Here we go! Three choc-anilla-berry milkshakes!'

Cassie's mum, Samantha, put the tray of frothy-topped loveliness on the table outside the deli and took a seat herself. 'Nice to see you and Florence paying us a visit, Ben,' she said with a warm smile.

Ben and his family had moved from interstate a few months earlier, and he'd been a bit stand-offish with the Bannermans, especially Cassie, to begin with. But their love of animals brought them together and now they were firm friends.

'Delicious milkshake – thanks, Sam,' said Ben happily. Sounds of loud slurping filled the air. Gladiator was purring contentedly on Cassie's lap. Florence and Ripper lay stretched out under the table, enjoying each other's company.

'I'm going to be busy here this afternoon, Cass, at least until your dad gets back,' said Sam.

'That's okay, Mum. We're going to head back to the park for a while. Mrs Stephens' ankle is still not great, so I said I'd take Rusty out for a bit of a run with Ripper.'

'Right, well I'd better get back to work,' said Sam. 'I know Dad's made his super-special lasagne for dinner tonight, in honour of our special guest; so don't arrive late. You won't forget Ruby, will you, Sarah?'

'I won't. We'll pop in on the way to the park and have a little play. I have the house key here in my pocket! And we'll be back in plenty of time for dinner. I love lasagne!' Sarah slurped up the last of her milkshake and Ben and Cassie followed suit. They were ready for action!

'Sarah only lives in the next street,' Cassie explained to Ben as they leashed up the dogs.

'And I'm in charge of my cat Ruby while Mum and Dad are away,' said Sarah proudly.

'She'll love the company after being on her own all day and she likes dogs! Well, most dogs anyway.' Sarah looked a little worriedly at Florence. She really was rather large. Florence's gentle smile set her mind at ease and off they all went.

Sarah used her key and pushed the door open. Everything was the same as it had been this morning, but the house felt different with no-one else at home. Sarah was glad that she had her friends with her. She was feeling a bit spooked. In her own house! Too weird.

'Hey, Ruby! I'm home, puss. Come on,

bubba, it's dinner time! ' she called out as they went in. 'That's funny. She usually comes running as soon as anyone opens the door. She loves company! Ru-by!'

'I bet she'll be all curled up asleep somewhere, enjoying the peace and quiet,' said Cassie. 'But don't worry, Ripper will find her!'

Ripper adopted his 'down to business' pose and started sniffing round the kitchen. In the living room, Florence attempted a 'down to business' pose too, but failed quite miserably and in her comical attempt, knocked over a large vase of flowers that had been sitting on the coffee table.

'Oops, sorry about that,' said Ben, grabbing the vase before it landed on the floor.

14

'Uh, Ben, maybe you and Florence might be better off checking out the garden?' Sarah suggested tactfully while grabbing a cloth and mopping up the spilled water. 'She's really an indoor cat, but there is a cat flap so she can go out if she wants to.'

'Or maybe,' added Cassie, slightly less tactfully, 'it might be time for you to go, Ben? Unless, of course, you wanted to join us for our sleepover? We could paint your toenails any colour you like! There'll be singing and dancing, cupcake baking . . .'

Ben was already heading for the front door with a grin. 'Okay, point taken, Cass. Come on, Florence, we know when we're not appreciated. See you later then.'

The door slammed shut after Ben and Florence. The girls grinned.

Sarah popped the flowers back in the vase. 'Good as new!' she said to herself as she dusted the orange pollen off her hands.

Suddenly they heard a single sharp bark coming in the direction of the kitchen. Cassie and Sarah ran towards the sound.

Chapter Three

In the kitchen, Cassie and Sarah saw Ripper sitting there calmly beside Ruby's food bowl.

'Oh, I thought he must have found her!' said Sarah, who was starting to worry. 'Never mind, let's keep looking.'

But as they turned to go, Ripper gave the same sharp bark. They both jumped.

'What's Ripper trying to tell us? Ruby's hardly touched the food I left out for her this morning,' said Sarah. 'It's odd that she'd leave that much behind. She's usually a good eater.'

'Yes, but look at this!' said Cassie.

Ripper relaxed and gently rolled his eyes. At last, he seemed to say, must I spell it out?

'There is nothing that looks more like cat-sick than, well, cat-sick,' said Cassie. 'Good boy, Ripper! If she has an upset tummy, chances are she's hiding out somewhere feeling sorry for herself.'

'But what if she's been sick all day and we never knew? Poor Ruby. Where are you, puss, puss?' Sarah was feeling anxious as she and Cassie renewed their search. They flew through the house checking out all of Ruby's favourite spots. There were a lot of them. Linen cupboard, toy box, bathroom sink, vegetable crate, snuggled against Dad's pillow, top of the bookcase, sunny spot halfway into Jack's closet . . .

Ruby seemed to have disappeared into thin air.

Then there was another bark, this time from the garden, and Cassie went running out the back door. Ripper was sitting beside a bush. Ruby, barely visible, was lying motionless beside him.

'She's here, Sarah!' yelled Cassie. 'Ripper found her.'

'Phew,' whispered Sarah as she ran down the stairs and into the garden.

Cassie wore a grim expression. 'She

19

doesn't look well,' said Cassie, stroking Ruby as Sarah reached her.

'What do you mean? Do you think she's still sick?' said Sarah, alarmed.

Ruby was very still and although her eyes were open and blinking every now and again, she didn't seem to be focusing on anything. She didn't even turn towards Sarah as she patted her gently.

'I think there's definitely something wrong,' said Cassie as the girls gently man-oeuvred Ruby out from under the bush.

Ripper, sensing the seriousness of the situation, kept watch on everything from a respectful distance.

Sarah was fighting back tears as she and Cassie felt all over Ruby's body for any sign of injury. There was nothing. No blood or cuts that would indicate she may have been in a fight. She didn't appear to have broken any bones and didn't really even seem to be in any pain.

'Oh, Ruby! I'm so sorry!' sobbed Sarah, giving in to her tears. 'Mum left me in charge, and now look! Poor puss!'

Cassie did her best to calm her friend, gently picked up the cat and placed her across Sarah's lap. Cassie was sure that it would make both of them feel better.

She ran back into the house and grabbed a cat box and fleecy blanket from the laundry and returned to Sarah as quickly as she could.

'Let's put her carefully in this and we'll get her straight to the vet. It's not far and Ben's dad will be there; he'll know exactly what to do.'

Chapter Four

Within a few minutes they'd arrived at the Abbotts Hill RSPCA clinic. The waiting room was busy but Margaret, the receptionist, took one look at the two girls' worried expressions and came over to them. She knew Cassie from her frequent visits and offers to help with everything.

'Cassie, what's happened? Who do we have here?' she asked.

'Hi, Margaret, this is Ruby. She's Sarah's cat. We've just found her like this in the garden. She looks really sick.'

At that moment Ben's dad, Dr Joe Stoppard, stepped out of the treatment room.

'Hello, Cassie. Oh, who's this?' asked the vet, casting an appraising eye over Ruby in her cat box. 'You'd better bring her straight through. Margaret, could you keep an eye on Ripper for a few minutes?' he asked, ushering Cassie, Sarah and Ruby through to the treatment room.

Sarah gave Dr Joe a quick rundown of the situation as he gently lifted Ruby out of the cat box. His hands moved quickly over the cat, but his voice remained slow and steady.

'So you hadn't seen Ruby since this morning, Sarah? What time was that?'

'I fed her as normal at about seven o'clock and then Mum and Dad dropped me at Cassie's just a bit after that.'

'But she looked and acted the same as usual? There was nothing different about her?'

'No, she was fine. But we noticed she had thrown up during the day and she doesn't seem to have eaten much,' said Sarah.

'She's not on any medication from the vet?' asked Dr Joe.

'No,' answered Sarah. 'She's never ill!'

All the time Dr Joe was examining the sick cat. He opened her mouth and looked under her tongue and down her throat; he opened her eyes and looked closely at each one with his flashlight. He checked her pulse and her temperature and gently ran his hands over every bit of her. Ruby was so floppy and soft and uncomplaining that it was hard to believe that she was a real cat at all.

'Well, there are no broken bones, but her stomach is pretty tender. I think the first thing we need to do is to get some fluid back into her body. There's a risk that she could become badly dehydrated and we don't want that to happen. We'll put her on a drip. That will regulate the amount of fluid going into her body.'

The girls nodded, listening carefully.

'I'm also going to take a sample of her blood and urine so that we can test it to see what the problem is here. The results will take a while to come back from the lab, Sarah. So we won't really know what the problem is until then. But I'm thinking that, so far, everything is pointing to the possibility that Ruby has somehow swallowed poison.'

Sarah gulped.

'But how could she be poisoned, Dr Joe?' said Cassie. 'Who would do such a thing?'

Dr Joe started fixing up a drip and administering medicine.

'I'm sure nobody has done it on purpose, Cassie. There are so many things that are toxic to cats and dogs, which are completely harmless to humans. Has Ruby had access to garden chemicals or anything like that?'

'Mum keeps all that stuff locked away in the cupboard,' said Sarah. 'I have two little brothers and they get into everything, so Mum has child locks everywhere!'

Dr Joe gently opened Ruby's mouth and deposited a tablet at the back of her throat. 'These tablets I'm giving her are charcoal. They'll soak up any poison that's left in her tummy. The only other thing we can do is keep her hydrated and wait. If we knew exactly what she'd eaten, we might be able to do more. But we won't know that until the blood and urine tests comes back.'

'Will she be all right?' asked Sarah quietly.

Dr Joe put a reassuring hand on Sarah's shoulder. 'We'll do all we can, but I'm afraid there are no guarantees. I'll stay in touch and let you know how we go.'

Cassie grasped Sarah's hand firmly, upset for her friend.

Chapter Five

'Ugh, that was awful!' said Sarah as they stepped out onto the street a few minutes later. 'She looked so ill! She's never stayed overnight at the vet before. It must be really bad.'

'You can't think like that, Sarah. Dr Joe is an awesome vet and if anyone can make Ruby well again, he can!'

They wandered back to the deli next door and brought Cassie's mum up to date with the events of the afternoon.

Sarah had felt brave in the clinic, but she could feel it wearing off now. She found herself wishing that her mum and dad were here so that she didn't have to feel so responsible.

'I just can't believe she was poisoned!' muttered Cassie. 'What could've happened? It's not as though Ruby is out and about all the time like some cats are. You've said Ruby's always at home.'

Sarah nodded her agreement.

'It's not as though your parents are in the habit of keeping bottles of poison all over the house, are they?' asked Cassie.

In spite of the solemn mood, Sarah found herself smiling at the idea. 'Nope.'

'Oh no!' exclaimed Cassie as she jumped out of her chair. 'I've forgotten all about Rusty. I promised Mrs Stephens I'd walk him today!'

'I'm sure she'll understand, Cassie,' said her mum. 'Just give her a call and let her know you could do it tomorrow instead.'

'I could I suppose, but poor Rusty will have been inside all day. He'll be driving Mrs Stephens nuts by now.' Cassie felt awful letting her down but felt too that she should really be looking after Sarah.

'I'll come with you,' said Sarah. 'I think I'll feel better outside. It might stop me from worrying about Ruby.'

Ripper gave a good long wriggly shake, and declared himself ready for a walk. He quite liked Rusty, even though he pretended not to. Blue heelers could be a bit bossy sometimes, but he knew deep down Rusty was one of the good guys.

Mrs Stephens was sorry to hear the news about Ruby and started telling them about a neighbour she'd once had who'd almost lost two cats to poisoning.

Sarah was trying hard not to listen, sure that it hadn't ended well, but Cassie was intrigued.

'So did she discover what had poisoned them?'

'Well, that's the funny thing!' declared Mrs Stephens. 'It turned out that she had poisoned them herself! By accident, of course. She loved salt. Whenever she made her lovely meat sauces she would pile on the salt, then give those sauces to the cats and they'd gobble them right up.'

Mrs Stephens loved telling a story and once she started, it was hard to get her to stop!

'She knew the cats liked the meat. But then they started getting sick and lethargic and she had to take them to the vet. The vet told her the cats shouldn't have so much salt in their diet. Simple as that. But, Cassie, those cats made a full recovery! And I bet Ruby will, too.'

Sarah gave a sigh of relief as Mrs

Stephens came to the end of her story and handed over Rusty's lead.

'Thanks so much for doing this, Cassie. Rusty and I both appreciate it. Another few days and my ankle will be right as rain again!' said Mrs Stephens as she shuffled back inside.

'See,' said Cassie to Sarah, 'those cats got better after being poisoned.' Cassie was determined to look on the bright side.

'Hmmm,' said Sarah, not completely convinced. 'But we only ever feed Ruby the best cat food or the same meat that Mum buys for us. She never gets leftovers, so it can't be salt.'

'It'd be good to know what it was though, wouldn't it?' suggested Cassie.

'Yes, it would,' agreed Sarah, perking up a bit. 'Dr Joe said he could do more to help her if he knew what she'd eaten!'

'Then let's find out!' declared Cassie.

Chapter Six

The girls were deep in conversation as they entered the park. So deep in fact that when they heard '*psssst*' they carried on walking. But when the '*psssst*' sounded a second time they stopped dead in their tracks.

'What was that?' said Sarah.

'*Psssst*, Cassie, Sarah!' They heard in a comical stage-whisper. 'It's me, Ben! Down here!'

Behind the lowest wall of the closest flowerbed, as far away from the dog-walking area of the park as it was possible to be, lay Ben. He was flat on his stomach with Florence lying quietly beside him.

'Is this some strange sort of obedience training?' said Sarah, turning towards Cassie for confirmation.

Cassie shook her head. She was as puzzled as Sarah.

'Cassie, is anyone looking over this way?' asked Ben.

'Uh, no. There's nobody here but me and Sarah,' said Cassie.

'You're sure?'

'Quite sure!' said Cassie. 'What are you doing down there?'

For the second time that day Ben seemed seriously embarrassed. He sat up slowly, still looking cautiously toward the dog area. Then he flicked his fringe back in an attempt to regain some small scrap of cool.

'Nothing. Just one of those things. I thought I dropped something . . .' Ben said, sounding very unconvincing.

'Okay then,' said Cassie, eyebrows raised.

'I think Florence and I have had enough running around for today. I might just carry on home,' said Ben.

Florence gave Rusty a jealous sniff on the way past. She didn't much like other dogs playing with her Ripper!

'Well, see you tomorrow then,' said Cassie. 'If your invisible stalker doesn't catch you first!' she added cheekily.

'So funny,' said Ben over his shoulder as he and Florence headed for the gate.

Cassie and Sarah looked at each other and began giggling.

While Ripper and Rusty rumbled and chased and ran and wrestled, Cassie and Sarah put their heads together. By the time the dogs were panting and ready for home, the girls had come up with a plan of action.

With a tired-out Rusty safely delivered back to Mrs Stephens, they retreated to the study in Cassie's house and turned on her mum's computer.

'Right!' said Cassie. 'Research!'

Sarah sat beside her with a notebook and pen, ready to list all the household things that might be toxic to cats.

There were a lot of them.

'But so many of these are things we encounter every day,' sighed Cassie.

'Like what?' said Sarah.

'Onion and garlic. They're both toxic to cats,' Cassie answered. The girls looked at each other, surprised.

'But we have those things sitting around in the kitchen all the time,' said Sarah.

'I guess they mean cooked onion that you might feed to your cat in leftovers,' said Cassie. 'Like Mrs Stephens' friend with the salt. But you said Ruby doesn't eat leftovers, so we can cross onions off the list.'

'Yes, but look,' said Sarah, pointing to the screen. 'What about chocolate? Tomatoes? Potatoes? Macadamias? Grapes? Avocado? Milk?'

Sarah carefully wrote them all down. 'I thought cats loved milk!'

'Lots of cats are lactose intolerant and milk upsets their stomach,' said Cassie, reading the information off the screen.

'Ruby never drinks milk, anyway. She prefers water,' remembered Sarah.

'This list goes on and on,' said Cassie, making a mental note of all the things she needed to check out round her own garden; chemicals, fertilisers, certain plants, detergents. It seemed endless.

Fifteen minutes later, equipped with Sarah's list and her house key, they set off back to Sarah's house.

Chapter Seven

'Okay then, Sarah,' said Cassie. 'Let's start over there at the bush where we found her. Is that her favourite place in the garden?'

'No, not at all,' said Sarah. 'She really prefers to be inside. Look at all the lovely things I've planted out here for her. Catnip and catmint – cats are supposed to love them. I thought they might tempt Ruby to come out more often to enjoy the sunshine and get some exercise, but they didn't really work. I guess she only likes the sunnier spots when it's not too hot.'

'There's no food left in the garden and the lid of the compost bin is shut, so she couldn't have gone rummaging round in there. Maybe the plants are more likely? Do you know the names of all these flowers, Sarah?'

'Not really. But you can look up the poisonous kinds on the internet. There'll be photos of each one. Here's the key. Mum's laptop is on the kitchen bench.'

'Good idea. And to save time, maybe you can check for any chemicals?' suggested

Cassie. 'Snail pellets, mouse or rat baits, fertilisers, anything like that. Your neighbour on that side has a pool,' she said, pointing. 'Ask them whether they might have left any chlorine lying around.'

Sarah nodded. 'That's a great plan of action, Cassie. I don't think Ruby ever leaves our garden, but I guess it wouldn't hurt to ask anyway. Let's get on with it!' she replied before running off.

Sarah quite enjoyed being busy for a while. It took her mind off Ruby and made her feel that she was doing something to help at the same time. When she asked her neighbour, he said he had never seen Ruby in his backyard. And in any case, they kept their pool chemicals under lock and key and didn't have trouble with rats, mice, slugs or snails, so there were no baits or pellets lying around.

Cassie was coming to the end of her search, too. The list of plants was a long one; azaleas, daffodils, lilies, irises . . . but none of the pictures she'd found online matched anything in Sarah's garden.

Even Ripper sensed the slump in mood and came to join the girls in the middle of the garden. They munched quietly on some biscuits Sarah found in the pantry before deciding that they'd really done all they could.

'It's getting late,' said Cassie, 'and I told

Mum we'd be in time for dinner. We should go. Come on.'

Cassie's dad had excelled himself in the kitchen and the lasagne was every bit as good as her mum had said it would be. But the mood at the table had been solemn.

'Would you like to ring your mum, Cassie?' said Sam as she cleared away the dishes. 'Let her know what's happened?'

'Do you think I should?' Sarah asked. She just couldn't decide what was the right thing to do. She really wanted to talk to her mum. She always made Sarah feel better and she'd realised that with all the excitement going on this afternoon, she'd forgotten her mum and dad wouldn't be there tonight to cheer her up with a hug and kiss before bed.

'But what if she wants to come home? They've waited a long time for this holiday and they were so looking forward to it. I don't want to spoil it for them!' Sarah confessed.

Sarah didn't think she could feel any worse than she already did, but the thought of telling her mum what had happened to Ruby was just too much. She even lost interest in her dessert. Lemon gelato!

'I think you should talk to her!' said Cassie, looking at the untouched gelato and making the decision for her.

Sam handed Sarah her mobile phone and gave her a big hug. 'Tell your mum that you've done everything you possibly could for Ruby, Sarah. I'll call her later for a chat too.'

Sarah went off to a quiet spot to talk to her mum. She felt happier already.

Chapter Eight

Later that evening, the girls were chatting quietly when they heard Samantha Bannerman shouting up the stairs.

'Cassie! Sarah! Dr Joe is here!'

They thundered down the stairs in their pyjamas without even considering the possibility that Ben might be there too.

He was.

'Oh! Hi, Ben,' squeaked Cassie, trying to hide behind the couch with Sarah rather than be seen in her pyjamas by a boy at eight o'clock in the evening.

To his credit, Ben only smirked ever so slightly. His dad, on the other hand, looked very serious. Cassie and Sarah glanced at each other and knew without being told that the news was not good.

'I don't have anything positive to report, girls.'

'Has she . . . died?' asked Sarah bravely.

'No, no, but she is unconscious.' Dr Joe looked over the heads of the girls at Cassie's parents and raised his eyebrows. Cassie turned around in time to see her mum's eyebrows go up too and then the slightest shrug; she knew even worse news was coming.

Ben's face was equally as grave as his father's.

'I'm sorry, Sarah, but there's a chance that she won't make it through the night,' continued Dr Joe. 'I'm afraid the results of the tests may just come too late. If we only knew what she'd eaten, there might be some hope.'

The girls quietly thanked Dr Joe and Ben for dropping in to let them know, even if the news was really bad.

Sam quietly showed the Stoppards to the door.

'Let's hope for the best, shall we?' said Cassie's dad as he came over and hugged both girls. 'Cats have nine lives. I bet Ruby has a few left, doesn't she?'

Sarah tried to smile. She really wanted to hope for the best but she couldn't, she just felt awful.

It was the quietest sleepover that Mr and Mrs Bannerman could ever remember.

Chapter Nine

It was morning, and before the girls were even dressed Ben was on the phone.

'Cassie! I think you and Sarah missed an important clue yesterday!' Ben announced excitedly. 'Something that Sarah said when we were at her house.'

'Well, tell me, Ben! It's too early for

twenty questions! What clue?' Cassie was not a morning person.

'She said that Ruby preferred to be inside the house. She's an indoor cat, but you said you spent the whole afternoon checking out the garden,' said Ben.

'So whatever poisoned Ruby might have come from inside the house!' concluded Cassie.

'Exactly. I'll meet you at Sarah's in ten minutes,' said Ben.

Despite her concern, Sarah had had a good night's sleep. She was optimistic about the search and she appreciated her friends'

efforts. If her cat could be saved, then Sarah would do what she could!

She and Cassie walked over to Sarah's house. As they reached the gate, they heard someone calling out, 'Cassie, Cassie!'

A little girl, already dressed for school, came running towards them, and both Cassie and Sarah recognised her as one of the tiniest kindergarteners at school.

'Hi, Amy!' said Cassie. 'You're up and about early. What's the matter?'

'I was just wondering if you've seen Ben this morning?'

'Ben Stoppard? No, but we're just on our way to meet him now. How do you know Ben?' Cassie was surprised.

'He's my reading buddy!' said Amy. 'I'm turning five tomorrow and I'm having a

party and I've been looking for Ben all week to give him this!' She held up a gorgeous handmade glittery party invitation. 'Do you think he might want to come?' she asked, staring up at them with big brown eyes.

'I'm sure he'd love to! Just leave it up to me!' said Cassie as she slipped the invitation into her pocket.

'Thanks, Cassie!' Amy chirped before skipping off, as happy as could be.

'Aha!' said Cassie in triumph, turning to Sarah. 'I think we have just discovered Ben's invisible stalker. She's real . . .'

'And tiny,' added Sarah.

'And totally unscary!' finished up Cassie.

Cassie and Sarah were still chuckling as they opened the door of Sarah's house.

CAT

Before they'd even had time to shut the door behind them, Ben appeared.

'Morning, Ben! Any invisible stalkers this morning? I thought I saw one lurking outside wearing our school uniform?' asked Cassie.

Ben looked very uneasy for a moment. They couldn't possibly know, could they? No, he was fairly sure Cassie was bluffing.

'Let's check the bathrooms first and the kitchen,' said Ben, quickly changing the subject.

They split up and spread out over the house but soon came back disheartened. The house was clean and tidy. The bins and toilets had their lids firmly down. The cleaning cupboards were well locked.

'This house is like a cat paradise!' declared Cassie as she stepped over a huge scratching post on her way into the living room. 'No wonder Ruby prefers to be inside. There are comfortable little cat nooks all over the place. I bet she loves this one!' she said, pointing to a small basket hanging under the coffee table. It was catching the morning sun and looked super-cosy.

'It's her favourite,' Sarah admitted. 'I think she likes this room best because it's quiet.'

'It smells nice, too!' said Ben.

'Actually, it does smell good. I hadn't noticed!' said Sarah. 'That'll be Mum's anniversary flowers. Dad always gets –'

The light-bulb moment hit all three children at the same instant.

A huge vase full of beautiful white waxy lilies. The flowers were gorgeous . . . and toxic to cats! They were one of the flowers Cassie had noticed when she was researching plants the day before. 'But why would she have eaten them?' said Sarah.

'She probably didn't. See that orangey dust? It's the pollen,' Cassie explained. 'It's almost as poisonous to cats as the rest of the plant. It's fallen onto the table and Ruby's water bowl is nearby. She probably didn't even taste it.'

Ben was already on his mobile phone, letting his dad know of their discovery.

'You know,' said Sarah, 'I don't think I'd make a very good detective. Florence knocked that whole vase over yesterday and I picked up the flowers without even thinking. The pollen was really hard to wash off! I had a bright orange clue on my hands all evening and didn't even realise!'

Chapter Ten

Nine o'clock was fast approaching and Ben, Cassie and Sarah were hurrying to get to school before the bell rang.

They'd had a busy morning already. They'd raced to the clinic to find that Ruby had survived the night. Even better, she'd regained consciousness. She still looked very ill and would need to stay on the drip for another few days.

'I can't tell you how lucky she is, Sarah,' said Dr Joe. 'Every part of the lily is poisonous to cats, and if she'd eaten more she would almost certainly have died. She must have swallowed the tiniest bit of pollen to be on the mend already. Great detective work from all of you. Can I suggest you tell your dad to buy roses for your mum next time?'

Sarah was overjoyed when Ruby seemed to recognise her. She even purred gently when Sarah stroked her tummy.

'It is going to be okay!' Sarah decided. 'I can't believe she's better!' Cassie's mum had promised to ring Sarah's mum and let her know about the improvement in Ruby's health.

'Oh, Ben,' said Cassie, digging deep into her pocket as they reached the school gates. 'Before I forget! Sweet little Amy Barker asked me to give you this.' She handed the party invitation to Ben with a big smile. 'It's on tomorrow after school and Amy was really worried that she might not see you before then, so I said I'd make sure it got to you. Should be great!'

Ben held the invitation as though it smelled really bad and his face turned the same colour as the paper. Really quite bright pink.

'How do you know Amy?' Ben was surprised.

Sarah interrupted. 'Cassie knows everyone in Abbotts Hill, Ben.'

Cassie nodded. 'It's true.'

'But she's been following me round for a week!' said Ben, finally letting his exasperation out. 'Ever since we did the Buddy Reading that day. She's driving me crazy! Everywhere I go, she's there! It's so embarrassing! She watches me play soccer, she comes running over to me every time I set foot in the dog park with Florence. My friends think it's hilarious, but there is no way I am going to a party with hundreds of five-year-old girls!' Ben sounded desperate.

Cassie and Sarah were doubled over in hysterics by the time Ben finished his rant.

'You may be happy to know Amy has a bit of a reputation for finding new friends . . . and sticking to them like glue,' said Sarah, wiping tears of laughter from her eyes. 'Amy was besotted with my brother Jack last term. But it was only a week before she found someone new to befriend.'

Cassie giggled. 'That's right. There was Tom Burrow from year four a few weeks ago. He had to turn down an invitation from Amy to go to the zoo.'

Sarah grinned. 'I remember now. He pretended he had chicken pox for the weekend.'

Ben looked abashed. 'Oh, I didn't realise,' he said. 'She is really sweet. And I feel better about the whole thing now that I know it's not just me.'

'Well, if you'd just asked us rather than running around looking like you were hiding from the secret police . . .' said Cassie cheekily.

The bell rang.

'Better go,' said Ben, running off to class, school bag and legs flying in all directions.

'Thanks for your help with saving Ruby,' called out Sarah to his retreating back.

'Any time,' he said, before almost careering into the vice-principal.

Cassie looked after him, thoughtful. 'The more I think about it, the more I realise Ben Stoppard behaves an awful lot like his dog.'

Sarah laughed. 'I've always thought that you and Ripper are like each other too.'

Cassie was about to get offended, and then she stopped. 'I guess you're right. We are quite similar.'

The girls hurried off to class, giggling.

'Tonight our proper sleepover begins, okay?' said Sarah.

'Pizza, gelato and a movie?' suggested Cassie.

'Count me in!' answered Sarah.

RSPCA 🐾

ABOUT THE RSPCA

The RSPCA is the country's best known and most respected animal welfare organisation. The first RSPCA in Australia was formed in Victoria in 1871, and the organisation is now represented by RSPCAs in every state and territory.

The RSPCA's mission is to prevent cruelty to animals by actively promoting their care and protection. It is a not-for-profit charity that is firmly based in the Australian community, relying upon the support of individuals, businesses and organisations to survive and continue its vital work.

Every year, RSPCA shelters throughout Australia accept over 150,000 sick, injured or abandoned animals from the community.

The RSPCA believes that every animal is entitled to the Five Freedoms:

Fact File

- freedom from hunger and thirst (ready access to fresh water and a healthy, balanced diet)
- freedom from discomfort, including accommodation in an appropriate environment that has shelter and a comfortable resting area
- freedom from pain, injury or disease through prevention or rapid diagnosis and providing veterinary treatment when required

- freedom to express normal behaviour, including sufficient space, proper facilities and company of the animal's own kind and
- freedom from fear and distress through conditions and treatment that avoid suffering.

HOW TO KEEP YOUR HOUSEHOLD PET SAFE FROM POISON

Many common household items such as food, plants and medicines are fatally toxic to our pets. It is important to be aware of the most commonly found poisons so that they are not kept within reach of your pet.

Rodent poisons and insecticides

These are one of the most common causes of pet poisonings. Poisons such as rat and snail bait should be used with extreme caution. If you must use rodenticides or insecticides, keep them safely locked up and only use them in areas of your property that are inaccessible to your dog or cat.

Medication

Many prescription and over-the-counter medications are toxic to animals. Paracetamol is a commonly found pain medication that is particularly poisonous to cats, even in tiny amounts. Never medicate your pet without the advice of your veterinarian and make sure that all medications are kept in sealed containers, out of the reach of your pets. Some pet medicines can also be dangerous to your pet if used incorrectly. For example, some flea-prevention treatments for dogs contain compounds that are highly toxic to cats.

Food
Some foods are toxic to your pets and should never be given to them. These include chocolate, onions and garlic (including products containing onion or garlic powder, e.g. baby food), tomatoes (for cats), macadamia nuts, raisins, grapes and products containing caffeine.

Feeding fat trimmings may cause your pet to develop pancreatitis, and foods such as raw fish, liver and sugary foods can lead to metabolic diseases when fed in excess.

Fact File

Avocado is toxic to many animals, including birds, dogs, mice, rabbits, horses and livestock.

Be careful not to feed your pets cooked bones, as these can splinter and can cause gastrointestinal obstructions and injury.

Common plants and mulch
Some common house and garden plants are deadly to animals if ingested. These include Lily species, Brunfelsia species (Yesterday-today-and-tomorrow) and cycad seeds. Cocoa mulch is also highly toxic if ingested.

Fact File

Fertilizers

RSPCA Australia recommends that owners take active steps to ensure that their dogs and other pets do not ingest any type of fertilizer material. If an owner suspects their dog or other pet has ingested fertilizer, they should contact their local vet immediately for further advice.

Fertilizer products generally contain varying amounts of nitrogen (N), phosphorus (P) and potassium (K) compounds. They may have additives such as herbicides, insecticides, fungicides, iron, copper and zinc. Because fertilizers are usually a combination of ingredients, the effects following ingestion may differ.

In general, fertilizers cause mild to moderate gastrointestinal irritation that may involve signs such as vomiting, diarrhoea, hypersalivation, lethargy and abdominal pain. In most cases the effects are self-limiting and can be resolved within 24-48 hours with supportive veterinary care.

RSPCA

Animal

Tales

COLLECT THEM ALL

COMING
SEPTEMBER 2012

**THERE'S SO MUCH MORE AT
RANDOMHOUSE.COM.AU/KIDS**